P9-CLD-956

The European Union

Political, Social, and Economic Cooperation

THE
EUROPEAN UNION

POLITICAL, SOCIAL, AND ECONOMIC COOPERATION

The European Union
Political, Social, and Economic Cooperation

POLAND

by
Heather Docalavich

Mason Crest Publishers
Philadelphia

Mason Crest Publishers Inc.
370 Reed Road, Broomall, Pennsylvania 19008
(866) MCP-BOOK (toll free)
www.masoncrest.com

Copyright © 2006 by Mason Crest Publishers. All rights reserved. No part of this publication may be reproduced or transmitted in any form or by any means, electronic or mechanical, including photocopying, recording, taping, or any information storage and retrieval system, without permission from the publisher.

First printing
1 2 3 4 5 6 7 8 9 10

Library of Congress Cataloging-in-Publication Data

Docalavich, Heather.
  Poland/by Heather Docalavich.
      p. cm.—(The European Union)
  Includes bibliographical references and index.
    ISBN 1-4222-0058-2
    ISBN 1-4222-0038-8 (series)
  1. Poland. 2. European Union—Poland. I. Title. II. Series: European Union (Series) (Philadelphia, Pa.)

  DK4040.D636 2006
  943.8—dc22

                                        2005015791

Produced by Harding House Publishing Service, Inc.
www.hardinghousepages.com
Interior design by Benjamin Stewart.
Cover design by MK Bassett-Harvey.
Printed in the Hashemite Kingdom of Jordan.

CONTENTS

THE EUROPEAN UNION

ICELAND
Reykjavik

GREENLAND SEA

BARENTS SEA

NORWEGIAN SEA

White Sea

RUSSIA

FINLAND
Tampere
Turku
Helsinki

NORWAY
Trondheim
Lillehammer
Bergen
Oslo
Kristiansand

SWEDEN
Stockholm
Gothenburg
Norrköping

Gulf of Bothnia

ESTONIA
Tallinn
Tartu

Gulf of Finland

Gulf of Riga

LATVIA
Ventspils
Riga
Liepāja
Daugavpils

Moscow

DENMARK
Aalborg
Helsingborg
Odense
Copenhagen
Malmö

BALTIC SEA

LITHUANIA
Klaipėda
Kaunas
Vilnius

RUSSIA

Minsk

BELARUS

UNITED KINGDOM
Glasgow
Edinburgh
Belfast
Liverpool
Manchester
Birmingham
London

IRELAND
Killarney
Dublin
Cork

Irish Sea
St. George's Channel

NORTH SEA

THE NETHERLANDS
Hamburg
The Hague
Rotterdam
Amsterdam
Düsseldorf
Cologne

Berlin
Leipzig
Dresden

POLAND
Warsaw
Wrocław
Kraków
Gdańsk

Kyiv

UKRAINE

BELGIUM
Brussels

LUXEMBOURG
Luxembourg

GERMANY
Frankfurt Main
Stuttgart
Munich

Plzeň
Prague
Brno

CZECH REPUBLIC

SLOVAKIA
Bratislava
Košice

English Channel

Paris

Nantes

FRANCE

Bern
SWITZERLAND
Geneva

Lyons

Bay of Biscay

Bordeaux

Toulouse

Gulf de Lion

Marseille
Nice

Milan
Turin

Venice

AUSTRIA
Linz
Salzburg
Vienna

Györ
Budapest
Szeged

HUNGARY

Ljubljana
Trieste
Zagreb

SLOVENIA

BOSNIA-HERCEGOVINA
CROATIA

Belgrade

YUGOSLAVIA

MOLDOVA
Chișinău

ROMANIA
Bucharest

Sea of Azov

BLACK SEA

VIGO
Porto
Bilbao

PORTUGAL
Lisbon
Faro

Madrid
Barcelona
Valencia
Seville

SPAIN

Florence
Rome

ITALY

Naples

ADRIATIC SEA

TYRRHENIAN SEA

Sofia

BULGARIA

MACEDONIA
Skopje

ALBANIA
Thessaloniki

AEGEAN SEA

Ankara

TURKEY

STRAIT OF GIBRALTAR

MEDITERRANEAN SEA

Rabat

MOROCCO

Algiers

ALGERIA

Tunis

TUNISIA

Tripoli

LIBYA

MALTA
Valetta

IONIAN SEA

GREECE
Kalamata
Athens

Sea of Crete

Lefkosia
(Nicosia)
CYPRUS
Lemesos

MEDITERRANEAN SEA

SYR

LEBANON

JOR

ISRAEL & THE PALESTINIAN TERRITORIES

Cairo

EGYPT

POLAND
European Union Member since 2004

Gdynia
Gdańsk
Elblag
Olsztyn
Szczecin
Bialystok
Bydgoszcz
Toruń
Gorzów Wielkopolski
Poznań
⭐ **Warsaw**
Lódź
Radom
Lublin
Wroclaw
Czestochowa
Kielce
Walbrzych
Zabrze
Sosnowiec
Katowice
Kraków

INTRODUCTION

Sixty years ago, Europe lay scarred from the battles of the Second World War. During the next several years, a plan began to take shape that would unite the countries of the European continent so that future wars would be inconceivable. On May 9, 1950, French Foreign Minister Robert Schuman issued a declaration calling on France, Germany, and other European countries to pool together their coal and steel production as "the first concrete foundation of a European federation." "Europe Day" is celebrated each year on May 9 to commemorate the beginning of the European Union (EU).

The EU consists of twenty-five countries, spanning the continent from Ireland in the west to the border of Russia in the east. Eight of the ten most recently admitted EU member states are former communist regimes that were behind the Iron Curtain for most of the latter half of the twentieth century.

Any European country with a democratic government, a functioning market economy, respect for fundamental rights, and a government capable of implementing EU laws and policies may apply for membership. Bulgaria and Romania are set to join the EU in 2007. Croatia and Turkey have also embarked on the road to EU membership.

While the EU began as an idea to ensure peace in Europe through interconnected economies, it has evolved into so much more today:

- Citizens can travel freely throughout most of the EU without carrying a passport and without stopping for border checks.

- EU citizens can live, work, study, and retire in another EU country if they wish.

- The euro, the single currency accepted throughout twelve of the EU countries (with more to come), is one of the EU's most tangible achievements, facilitating commerce and making possible a single financial market that benefits both individuals and businesses.

- The EU ensures cooperation in the fight against cross-border crime and terrorism.

- The EU is spearheading world efforts to preserve the environment.

- As the world's largest trading bloc, the EU uses its influence to promote fair rules for world trade, ensuring that globalization also benefits the poorest countries.

- The EU is already the world's largest donor of humanitarian aid and development assistance, providing 55 percent of global official development assistance to developing countries in 2004.

The EU is neither a nation intended to replace existing nations, nor an international organization. The EU is unique—its member countries have established common institutions to which they delegate some of their sovereignty so that decisions on matters of joint interest can be made democratically at the European level.

Europe is a continent with many different traditions and languages, but with shared values such as democracy, freedom, and social justice, cherished values well known to North Americans. Indeed, the EU motto is "United in Diversity."

Enjoy your reading. Take advantage of this chance to learn more about Europe and the EU!

Ambassador John Bruton,
Head of Delegation of the European Commission, Washington, D.C.

Twilight over Poland's Vistula River

CHAPTER 1

THE LANDSCAPE

Welcome to Poland, one of the largest countries in Central Europe. Bordered by Russia, Lithuania, Belarus, Ukraine, Slovakia, the Czech Republic, Germany, and the Baltic Sea, Poland's culture has been shaped by its central location and the ease with which people, ideas, and even armies have moved across the area.

Poland is the eighth largest country in Europe, covering an area of 120,727 square miles (312,685 sq. kilometers). Most of this area is low lying although there are some mountains to the south. The Baltic Sea lies to the north and provides Poland with easy access to Scandinavian and North Sea ports. Warsaw, the capital city, is situated in the center of the country, on the Vistula River.

A Sandy Coast, Rolling Plains, and Mountains

Stretching from coastal plains to mountain ranges, Poland can be divided into three major natural land regions—the Baltic coastal plain in the north, lowlands in the center, and mountains in the south.

The Baltic coastal plain is a low, flatland mass that lies along the Baltic Sea, extending across Poland from Germany to Russia. Marshlands, dunes, and tidal flats—coastal areas alternately flooded and drained by the tides—dot the coastline.

The region immediately south of the coastal plain is relatively flat. This low-lying region is marked by thousands of lakes. More than 9,300 lakes are scattered across the region. Wide river valleys divide the area into three sections—the Pomeranian Lakeland, the Masurian Lakeland, and the Great Poland Lakeland.

As these rivers cut through the lowlands, they provide fertile land for cultivation. The farmland of the plain is critical to Polish agriculture. Many Polish cities have developed along these riverbanks. Some of these cities have become important industrial and commercial centers, building upon the proximity of the rivers for the transport of goods and people.

South of the central lowlands are the uplands of Little Poland. This region is marked by striking up-thrusts of ancient rock, rich in minerals and coal. The coal, iron, zinc, and lead deposits found and mined here, near the old capital city of Krakow, have led to the growth of Poland's most important industrial region. The southernmost region of Poland is characterized by two mountain ranges, the Sudeten and the Carpathians, along the border with the Czech Republic and Slovakia. The Sudeten Range is somewhat smaller and features several granite quarries, while the Carpathians contain deposits of salt, sulfur, natural gas, and petroleum.

Rivers and Waterways

Poland is home to a number of interconnected rivers, canals, and lakes. Over the centuries, many of Poland's largest cities have developed along these water routes.

The most important river is the Vistula. Both a tourist river and a busy transport waterway, it flows from Slovakia in the south to the Baltic Sea in the north. The Oder is another river vital for transport, industry, and agriculture.

A TEMPERATE CLIMATE

Poland has a moderate, **continental** climate that is highly variable. Because of its nearness to the sea, Poland is affected by oceanic air masses from the west, cold air fronts from Scandinavia and the polar regions, and warmer air from the south. Instead of the more traditional four seasons, six different seasonal periods occur in Poland: a cold snowy winter lasting for as little as one or as many as three months, then a cold but drier period of alternating wintry and warmer weather, followed by a traditional sunny spring. Summers are warmer

The Vistula River

Poland's Tatras Mountains

with abundant rain and sunshine, followed by a sunny autumn. A cool, foggy period of humid weather signals the approach of winter.

TREES, PLANTS, AND WILDLIFE

Nearly 20 percent of Poland is comprised of grassy plains and meadows. An additional 27 percent is covered with forest. Add this to the marshlands and coastal habitats near the Baltic Sea and the mountainous regions in the south, and it is obvious why Poland is home to such a great variety of plants and wildlife.

Many migratory birds flock to Poland each year. Some of these include the highly endangered corncrake, which has been driven out of most areas of Europe due to intensive farming practices. The white stork also calls Poland home, with more of these birds found in Poland than in any other country in the world. Recent studies suggest that one of every four storks in the world is Polish.

Several different birds of prey also make their home in Poland. Among these, the white tailed eagle is perhaps the best known; with its impressive wingspan of almost eight feet (2.4 meters) and a sitting height of up to thirty-six inches (.9 meter), this is a predator to be reckoned with. Other birds of prey include the greater spotted eagle, European honey buzzards and the Eurasian hobby. The Nietoperek Bat Preserve, located in an abandoned World War II bunker system, is home to some of the rarest bat species in the world, including the barbastelle, the natterer's bat, and the brown long-eared bat.

The world's largest remaining concentration of European bison can be found in Poland's protected wildlife areas. The country is also home to a significant number of other large mammals, including the European elk, the grey wolf, and the European lynx.

Currently, Poland maintains twenty-three different national parks to protect its wealth of natural treasures. The richness and variety of its land nurtures Poland's modern government, just as it has for centuries.

QUICK FACTS: THE GEOGRAPHY OF POLAND

Location: Central Europe, east of Germany
Area: slightly smaller than New Mexico
  total: 120,728 square miles (312,685 sq. km.)
  land: 117,555 square miles (304,465 sq. km.)
  water: 3,174 square miles (8,220 sq. km.)
Borders: Belarus 253 miles (407 km.), Czech Republic 409 miles (658 km.), Germany 283 miles (456 km.), Lithuania 57 miles (91 km.), Russia (Kaliningrad Oblast) 128 miles (206 km.), Slovakia 276 miles (444 km.), Ukraine 327 miles (526 km.)
Climate: temperate with cold, cloudy, moderately severe winters with frequent precipitation; mild summers with frequent showers and thunderstorms
Terrain: mostly flat plain; mountains along the southern border
Elevation extremes:
  lowest point: near Raczki Elblaskir— –7 feet (–2 meters)
  highest point: Rysy—8,199 feet (2,499 meters)
Natural hazards: flooding

Source: www.cia.gov, 2005.

Poland's history lingers in ancient structures from the Middle Ages.

2 POLAND'S HISTORY AND GOVERNMENT

Poland has not always existed as the country it is today. For centuries, the nation suffered under the domination of foreign powers and the hardships of war. Today, Poland stands as a united, democratic country, and a new member of NATO and the European Union (EU). Poland is committed to peace and building good relations with other countries. However, Poland has traveled a long road to reach its current state.

EARLY POLAND

Ancient artifacts discovered on Polish lands suggest the area was home to **Neanderthals** and ancient tribal groups of **hunter-gatherers**. The area became more populated after the collapse of the Roman Empire as tribes from the south and west began to settle the area, probably seeking fertile farmland and freedom from the attacks of eastern tribes such as the Huns and Magyars.

By the tenth century, about twenty small states had been formed by various tribes. These groups included the Vistulans, Obodrites, Lendians, and Goplans. The most prominent group was the Polanes, or "People of the Plain," who settled the flatlands that still form the heart of Poland today. Originally a part of the Czech tribe, the Polanes eventually established themselves as a separate ethnic group and in time became the largest Slavic group. The region settled by the Polanes has been known as Poland ever since.

THE MIDDLE AGES

In neighboring Germany, Otto I, a strong Saxon emperor, founded the Holy Roman Empire in 962 CE. The Holy Roman Empire was a group of Western and Central European territories that were united by faith in the Roman Catholic Church. While there was only one emperor, each territory had its own individual ruler, appointed by the emperor.

In 966 Otto I granted the title of duke to Mieszko I, the leader of the Polanes. In exchange, the Polanes swore allegiance to the empire and began to convert the population to Christianity. By the time Mieszko died in 972, a strong alliance with the empire had been established, a substantial amount of additional land had been conquered, and conversion to Roman Catholicism was nearly complete. Mieszko's son Boleslaw continued his father's work and was crowned king of Poland by the emperor shortly before his death in 1025. The Kingdom of Poland was established and became one of the major powers in Eastern Europe.

In the centuries that followed, power shifted hands between different hereditary rulers as the kingdom faced **intermittent** warfare; some areas were lost to foreign invasion, while from time to time, new areas came under Polish rule. As the **Middle Ages** progressed, Poland saw a great influx of settlers from the west, mainly Germans who brought valuable skills and new ideas. The Germans also brought with them their legal practices, which, being considered more sophisticated than traditional Polish practices, were widely adopted. Poland, now with a **feudal system** firmly established, Roman Catholicism as the dominant faith, and Germanic customs and law becoming common practice, was

A medieval castle from Poland's past

now a fully integrated part of **medieval** Europe.

Although Poland now had firmly established ties to Western Europe, there were many important differences between life in medieval Poland and the remainder of Western Europe. Germans were not the only immigrants to move east during this period. Large numbers of European Jews, per-secuted during the **Crusades**, migrated to Poland as well. Poland welcomed these settlers and extended every protection of the law to the Jews. This included heavy penalties for the destruction of Jewish cemeteries and synagogues. Other important differences between Poland and the rest of feudal Europe included greater freedoms for the

peasantry and the larger class of **nobles** in Poland (nearly 10 percent of the population by some estimates) than in other areas of Europe. These differences helped fuel the rapid development of cities and commerce and set the stage for a new era of growth and prosperity.

POLAND'S GOLDEN AGE

By the end of the fourteenth century, Poland was still a relatively thriving nation despite political upheavals and periodic warfare. Seeking to improve political conditions, acquire new lands,

A church and monastery in Lezajsk, Poland

and enhance its military strength, Poland made a successful alliance with neighboring Lithuania. Lithuania was strong militarily and ruled large expanses of land to the east, including what is modern-day Belarus and parts of Ukraine. As a condition of the alliance, Lithuania converted to Roman Catholicism, and over the next century the resulting Jagiellonian Dynasty (named for King Jagiello, the first king of Poland-Lithuania who also ruled under the name Wladyslaw II) acquired land, wealth, and power.

The success of the Jagiellonian Dynasty can be traced to the distinctive features of its government, which was unlike the other European governments of the time. The large, landowning nobility had enough wealth and power to keep royal control in balance. Over time, a **parliament** was established, known as the Sejm, that was made up entirely of the nobility and had the power to pass laws, address grievances against the throne, and ultimately to elect a monarch. Although the Jagiellonians were a hereditary ruling family, they eventually began to expand the power of the Sejm as a means of ensuring their heirs would be elected as successors.

The result of this shared power was one of the most enlightened states to exist in Europe at the time. As other countries were torn apart by the religious strife caused by the **Protestant Reformation**, Poland enjoyed relative religious freedom. Although the majority of the country was solidly Roman Catholic, religious dissent was well tolerated, and Poland became a haven for Lutherans, Calvinists, and other religious groups being persecuted elsewhere. By the late sixteenth century, Poland also supported the world's largest population of Jews, who now had a thriving culture of their own and were prospering as bankers and business managers. Poland was ethnically and linguistically diverse as well, with ethnic Poles, Germans, Czechs, Slovaks, Belorussians, Ukrainians, and Lithuanians coexisting peacefully. Most ethnic Poles at the time were members of the nobility, who governed a mass of peasantry whose roots were not Polish or even wholly Catholic. Ultimately, however, this imbalance would result in ethnic conflict.

In the meantime, literature, music, and the arts thrived in this environment of prosperity and freedom. The Polish nobility commissioned works heavily influenced by the popular Italian styles of the late **Renaissance**. Italian-style architecture also flourished, and many examples are still visible in the old capital city of Krakow. The University of Krakow gained prominence as a world-class center of learning, and in 1543, Nicholas Copernicus became its most famous student as he revolutionized the study of astronomy forever.

Modern Poles remember this era as the golden age of Polish culture and identify their national love of freedom and democracy as originating in this period. While the large noble class and the middle class consisting of merchants, bankers, and skilled craftsmen did enjoy relative freedom and **civil liberty**, the large peasant class, however, still remained virtual slaves to the land they worked.

After the last Jagiellonian ruler died without a male heir, the government gradually evolved into the Polish-Lithuanian Commonwealth, or Noble's Commonwealth. Central power had eroded from the monarchy, and ultimately the country was governed completely by the legislature. Certain provisions in the constitution that allowed small groups of nobles to disrupt parliamentary procedures completely caused problems.

As the country faced external military threats and internal power struggles, the government eventually deteriorated. Over time, land was lost to Sweden, Russia, and the Ottoman Turks. Eventually, Poland came completely under the control of Russia.

NATIONALISM AND ROMANTICISM

In 1795, Poland was subject to the last of three partitions, where the neighboring powers of Russia, Prussia, and Austria completely divided the territory of Poland and wiped the Polish-Lithuanian Commonwealth from the map. While much of Europe condemned this action as a crime against Polish **sovereignty**, no country came forward to actively oppose the annexation. By the dawn of the nineteenth century, however,

new military developments encouraged Poles that their independence might one day be restored.

The French general Napoleon Bonaparte launched a series of aggressions and captured large portions of Europe. By 1806, he had dissolved Germany's Holy Roman Empire completely. The defeat awakened a sense of **nationalism** in the German territories. They banded together to fight against the French for Prussia, the largest German state. Poland's location in the center of Europe became very significant, and Napoleon promised to help restore an independent Poland— and he did in fact restore some **autonomy** to the Duchy of Warsaw. Although short lived, the Napoleonic era served as inspiration among **intellectuals** that a free and independent Poland was possible.

The artistic and intellectual climate of the day fueled the growth of nationalist movements in Poland. Nationalist movements swelled in popularity across Europe, and the artistic movement known as **romanticism** was a natural inspiration for this movement. Romanticism idealized patriotism and ethnic loyalty and promoted resistance against the **conservative** monarchies that imposed foreign rule on subject peoples across the continent. Arts and literature once again flourished, this time highlighting nationalist themes praising the glorious national past.

By the mid-nineteenth century, nationalist rebellions were occurring across Polish lands. The revolts were put down harshly, and actions were taken to limit the use of Polish language and cultural practices. Nationalist feelings also brought ethnic ten-

Architecture in Gdansk carries reminders of Poland's history.

The ruins of a concentration camp recall the horrors of Nazi occupation.

sions, and conflict arose between ethnic Germans, Poles, and Jews. As World War I approached, many different political groups were promoting Polish nationalism and independence.

WORLD WAR I AND THE POLISH REPUBLIC

World War I began on June 28, 1914, when Gavrilo Princip, a Serbian nationalist, assassinat-

ed Austrian archduke Franz Ferdinand and his wife, Sophie. Russia allied with Serbia. Germany sided with Austria and soon declared war on Russia. After France declared its support for Russia, Germany attacked France. German troops then invaded Belgium, a **neutral** country, since it stood between German forces and Paris. Great Britain then declared war on Germany.

The war put Russia on the opposing side from Germany and Austria, thus giving Poles political advantage, since both sides offered *concessions* of land and power in exchange for loyalty and recruits. Any perceived advantage was short-lived, however. Much of the war's heavy fighting took place on Polish lands, and two million Polish troops fought on both sides. Nearly half a million of those died. The *scorched-earth* policy pursued at the war's end left much of the region uninhabitable, and hundreds of thousands of Poles were removed to German labor camps during the war.

After the war, American president Woodrow Wilson supported an independent Poland as the thirteenth of his famous "Fourteen Points." In 1918, a newly independent Poland emerged, but it faced many great economic and political challenges. The new nation dealt with almost constant border disputes as boundaries were moved and redrawn across Central Europe following the war. The infant nation also had to contend with staggering amounts of war damage, a ruined economy, and dissatisfied minority groups who made up one-third of the country's total population. It is not surprising that as World War II loomed on the horizon, the new Polish government had failed.

NAZI GERMANY AND WORLD WAR II

Despite the multitude of internal problems, the greatest threat to Poland came from abroad. Poland allied itself with France for protection against both Nazi Germany and Soviet Russia. Poland also sought to further secure their position by signing **nonaggression treaties** with Germany and Russia.

Poland felt threatened because Germany was gaining power and rebuilding its military under the leadership of Adolph Hitler. In 1936, he formed an alliance with Italy and signed an anti-Communist agreement with Japan. These three powers became known as the Axis Powers. France, Great Britain, and the countries that were allied with them became known simply as "the Allies."

Hitler's stated goals of reclaiming German lands lost in World War I were initially accepted by the Allies, and a policy known as **appease-ment** was developed that granted a series of concessions to Hitler in hope of preventing another war. However, by 1939, the Allied policy of appeasement had granted Germany so much land that Poland was surrounded on three sides by Nazi possessions. When Poland refused Nazi proposals to join the Axis powers, Germany responded by invading Poland on September 1, 1939.

Polish forces were severely outnumbered and had no equipment to resist the state-of-the-art military technology employed by Germany.

Civilians suffered as Nazi planes bombed urban centers to weaken morale. In the end, despite fierce resistance, the Nazis overtook Poland.

Poland suffered greatly under Nazi rule. Not only were Polish Jews marked for extermination as they were throughout Nazi-controlled Europe, but ethnic Poles were persecuted as well. Nearly one million Poles were **deported** to work in forced labor camps in Germany. Measures were taken to

OSKAR SCHINDLER AND THE SCHINDLER JEWS

German, Catholic, bon vivant—all words that describe Oskar Schindler. There was little in his background to hint that he would play such an integral role in the survival of thousands of Jews in World War II Poland. After Germany invaded Poland, Schindler moved there to open a factory. To increase his profits, Schindler hired Jewish workers. German occupation meant that most of them had lost their prewar jobs. Desperate, they were the cheapest labor source Schindler could find. Schindler's accountant convinced some Jews who still had some wealth to invest in Schindler's factory. In return, they would be given a job and therefore less likely to be taken to concentration camps. Schindler treated his employees well.

After watching a German 1942 raid on the Jewish ghetto in Krakow, Schindler increased his attempts to help the Jewish population. He set up a "branch" of the Plaszow concentration camp in his Zablocie factory compound and compiled a list of the people he would need to run it—Schindler's List. The factory lasted for more than a year making defective bullets for the German army. Two years later, Schindler moved the factory—and most of his employees—to Brunnilitz.

Schindler escaped to Argentina with his wife and some employees after the war. Business venture after business venture failed, and Schindler left his family and returned to Germany in 1958. He spent the remaining years of his life traveling between Germany and Jerusalem.

During the last years of his life, Schindler was reportedly supported by those he called his Schindlerjuden—his children. The Israeli government honored him as a Righteous Among Nations, the highest honor given to non-Jews who risked their lives to save Jews during the Holocaust. After his death in Germany in 1974, his body was taken to Jerusalem for burial on Mount Zion in Jerusalem. He had told a friend that he wanted to be buried in Jerusalem—where his children were.

Today, there are more Jews alive worldwide who owe their lives to Oskar Schindler than remain in Poland.

The World War II concentration camp at Auschwitz, Poland

wipe out Polish culture and intellectual life. All universities and colleges were closed, and any Pole considered an "intellectual" was subject to execution. All education for Polish children beyond the primary level was banned. Poles were also conscripted for forced labor in Poland itself, and several labor camps were scattered across the country. All told, the Nazis killed approximately three million Polish Jews. An additional three million non-Jewish Poles were also killed or died as a result of Nazi occupation. In total, Poland lost more than 22 percent of its total population.

In June 1941, Hitler **reneged** on a nonaggression pact with the Soviets and invaded the Soviet Union. At war with the Soviets in the east and the Allies in the west, Hitler was outmatched. Soviets marched across Poland in late 1944, and the German government there collapsed. A valiant attempt by Polish resistance forces to liberate Warsaw before the Soviet advance was

KAROL WOJTYLA

Who? He's perhaps better known as Pope John Paul II.

Karol Wojtyla was born in Wadowice, Poland, near Krakow, in 1920. The future pope suffered much sadness in his childhood: his mother died when he was nine, and an older brother died when Karol was twelve. He himself was almost killed twice, first when struck by a streetcar and again when a truck hit him, which the athletic young man was able to overcome. In 1941, his father died, leaving Karol basically without a family.

In 1946, Karol Wojtyla was ordained a Catholic priest and served a church in Poland. After the communists invaded Poland and ordered no church services to take place, Wojtyla defied the edict and offered worship services. After becoming pope in October 1978, this first non-Italian pope continued his fight against communism. To many, Pope John Paul II was directly responsible for the fall of communism worldwide.

brutally put down by the Nazis, and by the time the Soviets arrived, Poland was unequipped for any further resistance. As Poland's boundaries were redrawn following World War II, the nation regained much of its hereditary lands, but it was now a communist **satellite state** of the Soviet Union.

COMMUNIST RULE

In the years following World War II, Poland suffered under communist rule. The country was in economic shambles, and an entire generation of Poles was poorly educated, since they had not been allowed to attend school under Nazi occupation.

Various groups made several attempts to rebel against the Soviet-controlled communist regime, but these were put down harshly. Because of its strategic location, Poland was a critical holding for the Soviets, so dissent could not be tolerated. By the 1970s, an attempt at **liberalizing** the economy had failed, and the country faced a crisis as the nation's debt spiraled out of control and even the most basic consumer goods grew prohibitively expensive.

By 1980, a group of anticommunist **dissidents** formed the independent trade union "Solidarity." Led by a shipyard electrician, Lech Walesa, the group promoted nonviolent protest as a means of political change and drew support from a wide variety of groups including the Roman Catholic Church, academics, as well as laborers and farmers. Solidarity eventually became

The Insurrection Monument in Warsaw

Open-air cafés in modern Krakow attract tourists

the leading force for resistance against communism. By 1981, the communists had outlawed Solidarity and imprisoned many of its leaders, which only served to gain the group even more popular support. The group continued to operate as an **underground** resistance movement, and by 1988, it had gained enough strength that the communist government began to negotiate openly with the organization. In 1990, the secretary general of the Communist Party resigned and was replaced by a **coalition** government led by Solidarity. In December of that year, Lech Walesa became the first **popularly** elected president of Poland.

THE POLAND OF TODAY

In the years since the fall of communism, Poland has begun to emerge from centuries of foreign domination and economic hardship as a thriving democracy. Looking back to the days of the Nobles' Commonwealth, the Polish people feel they have a heritage of democracy and civil liberty and are working to move forward and assume what they see as their legacy as an integral part of a unified and prosperous Europe. In achieving these goals, Poland has worked to make dramatic political and economic reforms.

They are also seeking to enhance their prominence in international affairs. Poland joined NATO in 1999 and became a member of the EU on May 1, 2004. These actions will have widespread effects on the nation of Poland, particularly its economy.

Modern-day Warsaw

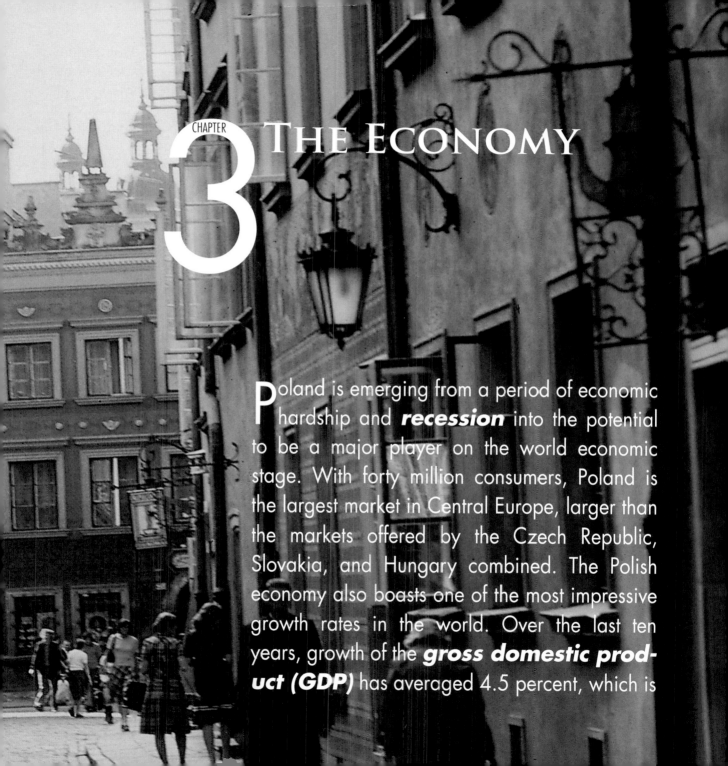

3 THE ECONOMY

Poland is emerging from a period of economic hardship and *recession* into the potential to be a major player on the world economic stage. With forty million consumers, Poland is the largest market in Central Europe, larger than the markets offered by the Czech Republic, Slovakia, and Hungary combined. The Polish economy also boasts one of the most impressive growth rates in the world. Over the last ten years, growth of the *gross domestic product (GDP)* has averaged 4.5 percent, which is impressive given that growth across the remainder of Central Europe for the same period averaged only 2.8 percent.

THE NEW ECONOMY

As Poland came out from under decades of communist control, the economy was in shambles. Large balances of unpaid foreign debt made borrowing difficult. And yet funds were needed to improve Poland's aged *infrastructure* before the nation could expect to see any real growth in foreign investment.

Privatization of industry and agriculture had begun before the collapse of the communist government; however, major reforms were needed to return to private ownership of businesses and to convert to a *market economy* after many years of state ownership. The new government instituted a program of "shock therapy" to revitalize the economy, and the dramatic reforms have paid off. Poland now has one of the most robust economies in all Europe.

QUICK FACTS: THE ECONOMY OF POLAND

Gross Domestic Product (GDP): US$463 billion
GDP per capita: US$12,000
Industries: machine building, iron and steel, coal mining, chemicals, shipbuilding, food processing, glass, beverages, textiles
Agriculture: potatoes, fruits, vegetables, wheat; poultry, eggs, pork
Export commodities: machinery and transport equipment, intermediate manufactured goods, miscellaneous manufactured goods, food and live animals (2003)
Export partners: Germany 32.3%, France 6.1%, Italy 5.8%, UK 5%, Netherlands 4.5%, Czech Republic 4.1% (2003)
Import commodities: machinery and transport equipment, intermediate manufactured goods, chemicals, minerals, fuels, lubricants, and related materials (2003)
Import partners: Germany 24.4%, Italy 8.5%, Russia 7.7%, France 7.1%, China 4.3% (2003)
Currency: euro (EUR)
Currency exchange rate: $US1 =.79€ (May 24, 2005)

Note: All figures are 2004 estimates unless otherwise noted.
Source: www.cia.gov, 2005.

INDUSTRY: THE MAINSTAY OF ECONOMY AND EXPORTS

Heavy industry is an important part of Poland's economy. The largest elements of the manufacturing sector are the automobile industry, iron and steel production, ship building, arms and weapons manufacture, and the chemical industry.

The increased demand for Polish products has enabled the Poles to rapidly develop a more modern infrastructure and dramatically increase productivity. The success of these industries

Tourists to the Baltic Sea

has been essential to the country's economic recovery.

One of the fastest-growing branches of Poland's manufacturing sector is the defense industry. As a member of NATO and as a border state of the EU, Poland has important military obligations that require a well-equipped, modern fighting force. Military electronics such as targeting systems, explosives, and the high-quality radar devices (produced by a company called Radwar), account for a large part of Poland's arms industry. In addition, the manufacture of heavy equipment, aircraft, and weaponry is expanding, and Poland has supply contracts all over the world.

The history of Poland's automotive industry goes back to the early 1930s when the first Fiat plant was built in Poland. Today, Fiat is still the largest automaker to do business in Poland, but Korea's Daewoo and General Motors have also invested heavily in Poland. Volkswagen and Toyota have parts assembly plants in Poland as well.

The Polish chemical industry is also thriving. Basic chemical products such as fertilizers, plastics, and dyes are produced by a number of Polish firms. The growth of the motor vehicle industry and the construction industry caused tremendous expansion in rubber manufacture, as demand for tires, treads for construction and military equipment, and PVC products rose accordingly.

A sheep farm in Poland

AGRICULTURE

Farming is a smaller but growing sector of the Polish economy. Poland is one of the world's largest producers of potatoes and rye. Other important food products produced and exported by Poland include pork, dairy products, poultry, and fruit. As conditions in Poland have improved, much of the food produced in Poland now meets the high standards required for the food to be exported to other EU nations. In addition, Polish farmers are counting on financial assistance from the EU to help build a more competitive agricultural industry. Agriculture is heavily **subsidized** by the EU's Common Agricultural Policy (CAP).

ENERGY SOURCES AND TRANSPORTATION

Poland is committed to implementing all aspects of the EU's energy policy. Environmental protection and **conservation** are among the most important factors of Poland's new energy policy, and it is critical to Poland's interests that the country develops new sources of energy to guarantee its future energy security. In addition to researching new and renewable energy sources, changes have been made in the way Poland uses its current energy sources. New natural gas pipelines have been built, linking Poland with Norway and Germany. Poland's electrical system was recently joined with the Western European grid, making it possible for Poland to sell its excess electrical power. Coal still remains the largest source of energy in Poland, but new advances have made this dependence on coal less damaging to the environment and more efficient. New sources of power such as **geothermal** energy and wind and solar power are slowly diminishing the large portion of Poland's energy provided by coal.

TRANSPORTATION

Highways, railways, waterways (both navigable rivers and canals located on modern ports and harbors), and airports make up Poland's complex transportation system. Five international airports connect Poland with the rest of the world, and Warsaw is quickly becoming the main transportation center for all of Central Europe. Poland's seaports are also vital transport centers, not only for Poland but for many of the landlocked nations of Central Europe as well. Polish ports are currently undergoing a period of restructuring to integrate shipping more smoothly with Poland's highways, railways, and air transport systems.

BUILDING A BRIGHTER FUTURE

Since joining the EU, Poland has continued to make important reforms to modernize the country's infrastructure and make Poland a major economic power in Europe. Now that the fundamental building blocks for economic success are in place, Poland expects to secure that growth by shifting its focus from an economy based on production to one based on information and technology. In time there is little doubt that Poland will be a truly equal partner with its partners in the EU.

Krakow's central square

4 POLAND'S PEOPLE AND CULTURE

Poland, home to nearly forty million people, is the largest country in Central Europe. The nation is ethnically *homogeneous*, with more than 96 percent of the population identifying themselves as Polish. The country is also 95 percent Roman Catholic, although only about 75 percent of those who identify themselves as

Traditional costumes at a Polish religious festival

Catholic actively practice their faith. Although other religious faiths in Poland are small in number, Polish worshippers today have complete freedom of religion. The Poles also have a strong national identity and are proud of their rich heritage and culture.

FOOD AND DRINK

Proud of their hearty appetites, Poles have traditionally preferred simple, meat-and-potatoes–style fare. **Western** influences in Poland today have brought some changes in eating habits. In Poland's

urban centers, people enjoy foreign foods such as pizza, pasta, and even Chinese and Mexican cuisine. For most Poles, however, the traditional favorites dominate. Meat, stews, potatoes, and cabbage are the staples of Polish cuisine. As in much of Central Europe, beer and wine are popular beverages. A variety of fruit-flavored liquors and vodka are also available.

EDUCATION AND SPORTS: AN EDUCATED AND ACTIVE PEOPLE

Poland is a nation that takes education very seriously. The literacy rate for adults is very high, and many Poles can converse in another language. The country has produced famous thinkers and athletes.

In Poland, education is **compulsory**, and every child between ages seven and sixteen must attend school. The school system, though, is quite different from most in North America. To begin, all children attend *Skola podstawowa* for six years. Next, students attend the *Gimnazjum*, or secondary school, for three years, after which they must complete a comprehensive exam. Depending on the student's interests and grades, there are several different options after completing Gimnazjum; each young person's path depends on whether she is interested in

vocational training or pursuing study at the university level.

When it comes to sports, Poles don't believe in just sitting on the sidelines. They go out and play themselves. Community centers offer sports complexes, pools, and athletic leagues for the public. Many different sporting events are held in Poland each year, although soccer is by far the most popular sport. If an important soccer match is being broadcast on television, the city streets may be deserted. Poland's most famous athlete is Adam Malysz, a world-champion ski jumper. Poland also boasts a proud Olympic history, with many Polish athletes winning medals over the years. Tennis, hockey, cycling, canoeing, sailing, swimming, skiing, and hiking are other popular sports.

ARTS AND ARCHITECTURE

Traditionally, Poland has been a land of grand architecture. History has not been kind to many of Poland's architectural treasures, however. In particular, the devastation caused by the two world wars destroyed many fine monuments and buildings of historic and artistic significance.

Nonetheless, some of Poland's most important architecture has survived or been painstakingly rebuilt or restored. Many of the best examples can be seen in Krakow, where many important Gothic and Renaissance structures have been preserved. The town of Kazimierz, on the banks of the Vistula River, is one of the best preserved medieval towns in Europe.

Quick Facts: The People of Poland

Population: 38,653,144 (July 2005 est.)
Ethnic groups: Polish 96.7%, German 0.4%, Belarusian 0.1%, Ukrainian 0.1%, other 2.7% (2002)
Age structure:
   0–14 years: 16.7%
   15–64 years: 70.3%
   65 years and over: 13%
Population growth rate: 0.03%
Birth rate: 10.78 births/1,000 pop.
Death rate: 10.01 deaths/1,000 pop.
Migration rate: –0.49 migrant(s)/1,000 pop.
Infant mortality rate: 8.73 deaths/1,000 pop.
Life expectancy at birth:
   Total population: 74.41 years
   Male: 70.3 years
   Female: 78.76 years
Total fertility rate: 1.39 children born/woman
Religions: Roman Catholic 96.7%, Eastern Orthodox, Protestant, and other 5%
Languages: Polish
Literacy rate: 99.7% (2003 est.)

Note: All figures are 2005 estimates unless noted.
Source: www.cia.org, 2005.

pride of the nineteenth century, portrayed important events from Poland's history on a monumental scale. In addition to painting, Poles have made significant contributions in the fields of sculpture, photography, and cinema. Roman Polanski, one of the most celebrated directors of all time, is hailed as the father of Polish cinema.

Music and Literature: A Source of Pride

Literary works written in the Polish **vernacular** date back to before the fourteenth century. Throughout the centuries Polish literature flourished, much of it in the form of poetry. Examples of important Polish literature can be found in almost all the famous literary styles that occurred in Europe, notably Renaissance, Baroque, and Neo-Classicist works.

Poland's great heyday of Romanticist literature occurred in the nineteenth century and inspired the nationalist ambitions of the Polish people. Henryk Sienkiewicz won the Nobel Prize for Literature for his book *Quo Vadis*, written in 1905. In the turmoil of the twenti-

Poles are proud of their contributions to the visual arts as well. Perhaps the most famous contribution to the visual arts was Jan Matejko's illustrious school of Historicist painting. These paintings, inspired by the romanticism and nationalist

A Good Friday procession

An accordian player performs polka music.

eth century, many Polish writers continued to publish important works in **exile**, having fled the destruction of the world wars or the oppression of the communist regime. Another Nobel Prize winner, Czeslaw Milosz, was one of these *émigré* writers.

In music, Poles have made important contributions as well. The romanticism that gripped nineteenth-century Poland inspired the music of Frédéric Chopin, which is now among the best-loved classical music of all time. Chopin in turn stimulated the nationalist aspirations of his fellow Poles by introducing elements of traditional Polish folk music into his works. The same period produced the growth of the Polish opera, with Stanislaw Moniuszko as its most recognized composer.

Folk music still occupies a prominent place in Polish culture. People around the world recognize traditional Polish dance music such as the polka and the mazurka. Today, tourists and locals alike frequent the many cultural festivals that highlight Polish music and dancing.

Modern music also has a prominent place in today's Poland. Poland has always been very open to new styles of music and even before the fall of communism, Western popular music had gained an audience in Poland. While pop music is popular, it is dominated by the Polish love of hard rock and hip-hop styles of music. Many Polish artists are producing their own varieties of hip-hop and rock music. Polish jazz also has a small but dedicated following. Jazz festivals feature this blend of a uniquely American musical style fused with compositions characteristically Polish in flavor.

MARIE CURIE

Poles are not just famous for artistic, musical, and literary achievements. Marie Sklodowska Curie, the first person to win or share two Nobel Prizes, was born in Warsaw, Poland, in 1867.

After graduating from high school, she was unable to study at any Russian or Polish universities because she was female. So, Marie worked as a governess for several years. Eventually, with financial assistance from an older sister, Marie was able to attend the Sorbonne, in Paris, where she studied chemistry and physics. It was there that she met her husband, Pierre Curie, and together, they studied radioactive materials, discovering radium and polonium.

Curie died from leukemia in 1934, most likely caused by her long-term exposure to radiation in her work. A year after her death, her eldest daughter won the Noble Prize for Chemistry.

Gdansk on the Motlawa River

5 THE CITIES

Today's Poland is an urban society. Much of the population lives in cities and towns, and the standard of living has improved with the economic growth that followed the collapse of the communist government. Modern Polish families tend to be quite small; couples usually have only one child, and many have none.

Most of Poland's cities are medium-sized or small; only a few large cities exist. Most Polish cities are centuries old and built upon ancient trade routes and waterways. Today, modern structures coexist with ancient monuments, Gothic churches, and Soviet-era factories and apartment complexes.

Polish cities also consciously promote a rich cultural life. Many towns subsidize theater, music festivals, and art exhibits.

VARIED POPULATION DENSITY

Poland is comprised of sixteen provinces whose population densities vary greatly. The most densely populated are those that include major urban centers like Warsaw, Lodz, and Krakow. Agricultural areas are the least populated, with many families working their own small farms in rural communities.

WARSAW: THE CAPITAL

Warsaw, located on the Vistula River, near the center of the country, is Poland's capital and most-populated city. The city is home to many important industries, sixty-six different colleges and universities, and more than thirty different theater companies, including the National Theater and Opera and the Philharmonic National Orchestra. Warsaw is perhaps most remarkable for the fact that it has survived for so long. The city suffered assaults in 1655 and 1794. The city was then severely bombed during the German invasion of Poland in World War II, and after the retreat of German troops in 1944, Hitler ordered the entire

city to be destroyed. Eighty-five percent of the city was completely flattened. Nevertheless, the city continued as Poland's capital, and today Warsaw is the center of Polish political, economic, and cultural life. Many of the old structures have been rebuilt, and the historic Old Town of Warsaw is on the UNESCO World Heritage List.

LODZ: A RICH METROPOLIS

Poland's second-most populated city, Lodz, is home to many of Poland's most important industries. The city is now a thriving metropolis, boasting not only a number of important industries but several parks, a zoo, botanical gardens, and one of Poland's best-known art museums. The city is also home to a number of important eighteenth- and nineteenth-century historical structures. The University of Lodz and the Technical University of Lodz draw in students from all over Poland.

KRAKOW: A HISTORIC TREASURE

Situated in the south of Poland, Krakow, once the nation's capital, is the nation's third-largest city. Settlement of Krakow dates back to the fourth cen-

Old market house in Krakow

tury, and the city is now considered the cultural heart of Poland. It is home to Poland's oldest university, and today hosts eighteen different universities, colleges, and technical schools. The city also has twenty-eight museums, and numerous concert halls and theaters. Tourists are attracted to the city's rich architecture; structures can be found in Krakow representing Renaissance, Baroque and Gothic styles.

The old harbor in Gdansk

Krakow also hosts many important cultural events such as the Festival of Short Feature Films, the Biennial of Graphics, and the Jewish Culture Festival.

POZNAN: AN INDUSTRIAL CENTER

Poznan is the fourth-largest industrial center in Poland. Located in the western part of the country on the Warta River, Poznan is a vital center for trade, industry, and education. Poznan also has historic significance; its cathedral is the earliest surviving church in Poland and contains the tombs of several early Polish rulers. Poznan is now the major center for trade with Germany and is home to a number of industries as well as important colleges and universities.

GDANSK: A HARBOR CITY

With a thriving shipbuilding industry, Gdansk is Poland's principal seaport. It is a crucial transport center not only for Poland but for neighboring countries with no seaports of their own. In addition to shipping and ship building, the port city is also home to a large share of Poland's chemical and electronics industries. Gdansk has ten different colleges and universities and holds many important cultural events each year.

The EU flag

6

THE FORMATION OF THE EUROPEAN UNION

The EU is an economic and political confederation of twenty-five European nations. Member countries abide by common foreign and security policies and cooperate on judicial and domestic affairs. The confederation, however, does not replace existing states or governments. Each of the twenty-five member states is **_autonomous_**, but they have all agreed to establish some common institutions and to hand over some of their own decision-making powers to these international bodies. As a result, decisions on matters that interest all member states can be made democratically, accommodating everyone's concerns and interests.

Today, the EU is the most powerful regional organization in the world. It has evolved from a primarily economic organization to an increasingly political one. Besides promoting economic cooperation, the EU requires that its members uphold fundamental values of peace and **solidarity**, human dignity, freedom, and equality. Based on the principles of democracy and the rule of law, the EU respects the culture and organizations of member states.

HISTORY

The seeds of the EU were planted more than fifty years ago in a Europe reduced to smoking piles of rubble by two world wars. European nations suffered great financial difficulties in the postwar period. They were struggling to get back on their feet and realized that another war would cause further hardship. Knowing that internal conflict was hurting all of Europe, a drive began toward European cooperation.

France took the first historic step. On May 9, 1950 (now celebrated as Europe Day), Robert Schuman, the French foreign minister, proposed the coal and steel industries of France and West Germany be coordinated under a single supranational authority. The proposal, known as the Treaty of Paris, attracted four other countries—Belgium, Luxembourg, the Netherlands, and Italy—and resulted in the 1951 formation of the European Coal and Steel Community (ECSC). These six countries became the founding members of the EU.

In 1957, European cooperation took its next big leap. Under the Treaty of Rome, the European Economic Community (EEC) and the European Atomic Energy Community (EURATOM) were formed. Informally known as the Common Market, the EEC promoted joining the national economies into a single European economy. The 1965 Treaty of Brussels (more commonly referred to as the Merger Treaty) united these various treaty organizations under a single umbrella, the European Community (EC).

In 1992, the Maastricht Treaty (also known as the Treaty of the European Union) was signed in Maastricht, the Netherlands, signaling the birth of the EU as it stands today. **Ratified** the following year, the Maastricht Treaty provided for a central banking system, a common currency (the euro) to replace the national currencies, a legal definition of the EU, and a framework for expanding the

The EU's united economy has allowed it to become a worldwide financial power.

EU's political role, particularly in the area of foreign and security policy.

By 1993, the member countries completed their move toward a single market and agreed to participate in a larger common market, the European Economic Area, established in 1994.

The EU, headquartered in Brussels, Belgium, reached its current member strength in spurts. In

© BCE ECB EZB EKT EKP 2002

© BCE ECB EZB EKT EKP 2002

© BCE ECB EZB EKT EKP 2002

© BCE ECB EZB EKT EKP 2002

The euro, the EU's currency

1973, Denmark, Ireland, and the United Kingdom joined the six founding members of the EC. They were followed by Greece in 1981, and Portugal and Spain in 1986. The 1990s saw the unification of the two Germanys, and as a result, East Germany entered the EU fold. Austria, Finland, and Sweden joined the EU in 1995, bringing the total number of member states to fifteen. In 2004, the EU nearly doubled its size when ten countries—Cyprus, the Czech Republic, Estonia, Hungary, Latvia, Lithuania, Malta, Poland, Slovakia, and Slovenia—became members.

THE EU FRAMEWORK

The EU's structure has often been compared to a "roof of a temple with three columns." As established by the Maastricht Treaty, this three-pillar framework encompasses all the policy areas—or pillars—of European cooperation. The three pillars of the EU are the European Community, the Common Foreign and Security Policy (CFSP), and Police and Judicial Co-operation in Criminal Matters.

QUICK FACTS: THE EUROPEAN UNION

Number of Member Countries: 25
Official Languages: 20—Czech, Danish, Dutch, English, Estonian, Finnish, French, German, Greek, Hungarian, Italian, Latvian, Lithuanian, Maltese, Polish, Portuguese, Slovak, Slovenian, Spanish, and Swedish; additional language for treaty purposes: Irish Gaelic.
Motto: *In Varietate Concordia* (United in Diversity)
European Council's President: Each member state takes a turn to lead the council's activities for 6 months.
European Commission's President: José Manuel Barroso (Portugal)
European Parliament's President: Josep Borrell (Spain)
Total Area: 1,502,966 square miles (3,892,685 sq. km.)
Population: 454,900,000
Population Density: 302.7 people/square mile (116.8 people/sq. km.)
GDP: €9.61.1012
Per Capita GDP: €21,125
Formation:
- Declared: February 7, 1992, with signing of the Maastricht Treaty
- Recognized: November 1, 1993, with the ratification of the Maastricht Treaty

Community Currency: Euro. Currently 12 of the 25 member states have adopted the euro as their currency.
Anthem: "Ode to Joy"
Flag: Blue background with 12 gold stars arranged in a circle
Official Day: Europe Day, May 9.

Source: europa.eu.int

Pillar One

The European Community pillar deals with economic, social, and environmental policies. It is a body consisting of the European Parliament, European Commission, European Court of Justice, Council of the European Union, and the European Courts of Auditors.

Pillar Two

The idea that the EU should speak with one voice in world affairs is as old as the European integration process itself. Toward this end, the Common Foreign and Security Policy (CFSP) was formed in 1993.

PILLAR THREE

The cooperation of EU member states in judicial and criminal matters ensures that its citizens enjoy the freedom to travel, work, and live securely and safely anywhere within the EU. The third pillar—Police and Judicial Co-operation in Criminal Matters—helps to protect EU citizens from international crime and to ensure equal access to justice and fundamental rights across the EU.

The flags of the EU's nations:

top row, left to right
Belgium, the Czech Republic, Denmark, Germany, Estonia, Greece

second row, left to right
Spain, France, Ireland, Italy, Cyprus, Latvia

third row, left to right
Lithuania, Luxembourg, Hungary, Malta, the Netherlands, Austria

bottom row, left to right
Poland, Portugal, Slovenia, Slovakia, Finland, Sweden, United Kingdom

ECONOMIC STATUS

As of May 2004, the EU had the largest economy in the world, followed closely by the United States. But even though the EU continues to enjoy a trade surplus, it faces the twin problems of high unemployment rates and *stagnancy*.

The 2004 addition of ten new member states is expected to boost economic growth. EU membership is likely to stimulate the economies of these relatively poor countries. In turn, their prosperity growth will be beneficial to the EU.

THE EURO

The EU's official currency is the euro, which came into circulation on January 1, 2002. The shift to the euro has been the largest monetary changeover in the world. Twelve countries—Belgium, Germany, Greece, Spain, France, Ireland, Italy, Luxembourg, the Netherlands, Finland, Portugal, and Austria—have adopted it as their currency.

SINGLE MARKET

Within the EU, laws of member states are harmonized and domestic policies are coordinated to create a larger, more-efficient single market.

The chief features of the EU's internal policy on the single market are:

- free trade of goods and services

- a common EU competition law that controls anticompetitive activities of companies and member states

- removal of internal border control and harmonization of external controls between member states

- freedom for citizens to live and work anywhere in the EU as long as they are not dependent on the state

- free movement of **capital** between member states

- harmonization of government regulations, corporation law, and trademark registration

- a single currency

- coordination of environmental policy

- a common agricultural policy and a common fisheries policy

- a common system of indirect taxation, the value-added tax (VAT), and common customs duties and **excise**

- funding for research

- funding for aid to disadvantaged regions

The EU's external policy on the single market specifies:

- a common external **tariff** and a common position in international trade negotiations

- funding of programs in other Eastern European countries and developing countries

COOPERATION AREAS

EU member states cooperate in other areas as well. Member states can vote in European Parliament elections. Intelligence sharing and cooperation in criminal matters are carried out through EUROPOL and the Schengen Information System.

The EU is working to develop common foreign and security policies. Many member states are resisting such a move, however, saying these are sensitive areas best left to individual member states. Arguing in favor of a common approach to security and foreign policy are countries like France and Germany, who insist that a safer and more secure Europe can only become a reality under the EU umbrella.

One of the EU's great achievements has been to create a boundary-free area within which people, goods, services, and money can move around freely; this ease of movement is sometimes called "the four freedoms." As the EU grows in size, so do the challenges facing it—and yet its fifty-year history has amply demonstrated the power of cooperation.

Europe is proud of its "bright idea," a union with economic and political power.

The EU believes that it can use its power to act as a "lighthouse" for the rest of the world.

KEY EU INSTITUTIONS

Five key institutions play a specific role in the EU.

THE EUROPEAN PARLIAMENT

The European Parliament (EP) is the democratic voice of the people of Europe. Directly elected every five years, the Members of the European Parliament (MEPs) sit not in national **blocs** but in political groups representing the seven main political parties of the member states. Each group reflects the political ideology of the national parties to which its members belong. Some MEPs are not attached to any political group.

COUNCIL OF THE EUROPEAN UNION

The Council of the European Union (formerly known as the Council of Ministers) is the main leg-

islative and decision-making body in the EU. It brings together the nationally elected representatives of the member-state governments. One minister from each of the EU's member states attends council meetings. It is the forum in which government representatives can assert their interests and reach compromises. Increasingly, the Council of the European Union and the EP are acting together as colegislators in decision-making processes.

EUROPEAN COMMISSION

The European Commission does much of the day-to-day work of the EU. Politically independent, the commission represents the interests of the EU as a whole, rather than those of individual member states. It drafts proposals for new European laws, which it presents to the EP and the Council of the European Union. The European Commission makes sure EU decisions are implemented properly and supervises the way EU funds are spent. It also sees that everyone abides by the European treaties and European law.

The EU member-state governments choose the European Commission president, who is then approved by the EP. Member states, in consultation with the incoming president, nominate the other European Commission members, who must also be approved by the EP. The commission is appointed for a five-year term, but can be dismissed by the EP. Many members of its staff work in Brussels, Belgium.

COURT OF JUSTICE

Headquartered in Luxembourg, the Court of Justice of the European Communities consists of one independent judge from each EU country. This court ensures that the common rules decided in the EU are understood and followed uniformly by all the members. The Court of Justice settles disputes over how EU treaties and legislation are interpreted. If national courts are in doubt about how to apply EU rules, they must ask the Court of Justice. Individuals can also bring proceedings against EU institutions before the court.

COURT OF AUDITORS

EU funds must be used legally, economically, and for their intended purpose. The Court of Auditors, an independent EU institution located in Luxembourg, is responsible for overseeing how EU money is spent. In effect, these auditors help European taxpayers get better value for the money that has been channeled into the EU.

OTHER IMPORTANT BODIES

1. European Economic and Social Committee: expresses the opinions of organized civil society on economic and social issues

2. Committee of the Regions: expresses the opinions of regional and local authorities

3. European Central Bank: responsible for monetary policy and managing the euro

4. European Ombudsman: deals with citizens' complaints about mismanagement by any EU institution or body

5. European Investment Bank: helps achieve EU objectives by financing investment projects

Together with a number of agencies and other bodies completing the system, the EU's institutions have made it the most powerful organization in the world.

EU MEMBER STATES

In order to become a member of the EU, a country must have a stable democracy that guarantees the rule of law, human rights, and protection of minorities. It must also have a functioning market economy as well as a civil service capable of applying and managing EU laws.

The EU provides substantial financial assistance and advice to help candidate countries prepare themselves for membership. As of October 2004, the EU has twenty-five member states. Bulgaria and Romania are likely to join in 2007, which would bring the EU's total population to nearly 500 million.

In December 2004, the EU decided to open negotiations with Turkey on its proposed membership. Turkey's possible entry into the EU has been fraught with controversy. Much of this controversy has centered on Turkey's human rights record and the divided island of Cyprus. If allowed to join the EU, Turkey would be its most-populous member state.

The 2004 expansion was the EU's most ambitious enlargement to date. Never before has the EU embraced so many new countries, grown so much in terms of area and population, or encompassed so many different histories and cultures. As the EU moves forward into the twenty-first century, it will undoubtedly continue to grow in both political and economic strength.

Poland's countryside

7 POLAND IN THE EUROPEAN UNION

Ten new member nations were admitted to the EU in May of 2004. These nations were Poland, Cyprus, Estonia, Hungary, Latvia, Lithuania, Malta, Slovakia, the Czech Republic, and Slovenia. As a relatively new member of the EU, Poland is making important strides to ensure its status as an equal partner.

POLAND AND EU ACCESSION

In 2003, following more than a decade of sweeping economic and political reforms, Poles voted for membership in the EU in a historic **referendum**. Although national polling showed that a few Poles had concerns about joining the EU, the majority felt that tapping into the resources of a wider Europe would bring their new country more advantages than disadvantages. The process of joining the EU, called accession, requires potential member states to adopt common policies on a wide variety of issues—from trade and commerce, to environmental protection and human rights. From the earliest days of the democratic government, one of the most important goals of Poland's economic and political reforms was to establish greater ties with Western Europe and ultimately obtain EU membership.

DIFFERING VIEWS OF A UNITED EUROPE

Public opinion in Europe remains divided over the amount of decision-making control member nations should surrender to the EU. Most Poles want to surrender a minimum of sovereignty. Concern has been expressed that, as a nation who has only recently gained a democratically elected legislative body, the Polish voting public should have more control over legislation being passed than the European Parliament in Brussels. Currently, Poland and many of the other new EU states support a policy termed intergovernmental-

Peasants in the Tatra Mountains

ism—a governmental approach in which member states must decide on policy by unanimous agreement. Poland remains concerned that their status as a new member of the EU, and their slight economic disadvantage, put their interests behind those of larger countries like Germany and France in EU decision making.

Others, primarily in the larger EU countries, feel strongly that the greatest opportunities for growth can be found within the framework of a strongly united Europe. Supporters of supranationalism—a governmental approach in which EU member states would be bound by decisions based on majority rule, believe that the benefits of having common policies for defense, treaty negotiation, and trade far outweigh the individual interests of separate member states.

Poland's Tatra Mountains

Strengthening Europe's Defense

One result of the latest EU expansion is that the outlying borders of the union have changed. As a border nation, Poland takes its responsibility for the defense of Europe seriously. This is especially critical as the borders of a united Europe continue to stretch toward more unstable nations to the east. Poland has dramatically increased its military expenditures to meet this challenge. Research funds from the EU are being sought to improve surveillance technology and to enhance manpower necessary to ensure border security.

Poland also believes there is security to be found in prosperity. Polish citizens have expressed strong support for the further expansion of the EU to include the Baltic States and other former Soviet countries to the east. Poland believes that by strengthening the economies of these nations and helping them to meet the standards required for accession to the EU, the region will be stabilized politically, helping to ensure lasting peace.

Active Support for CAP

Poland is an active supporter of the EU's CAP. The program's aim is to provide farmers with a reasonable standard of living and consumers with wholesome food at reasonable prices. Today, CAP's focuses are food safety, environmental protection, and value for money.

Modernization of farms, rural development, and fair payments to farmers are the top priorities of the EU agenda, and correspond nicely to the concerns of Poland's agricultural and food-processing industries. As intensive farming methods across Europe have sparked concerns about the environment and animal welfare, Poland has traditionally employed more environmentally friendly methods of production than many of their competitors in Western Europe. Polish farmers have already begun to see the benefits of EU membership through increased subsidies for agriculture and expanded markets for their products.

Research is another important priority for Polish agriculture. The EU funds a great deal of research into **sustainable** production, environmental conservation, and plant and animal diseases. Poland is seeking to take advantage of these funds through an increase in agricultural research.

Benefits of EU Membership

EU membership is already making an impact on many different areas of Polish life. Poland has worked hard to make the dramatic economic and political changes that were necessary to be eligible for EU membership, but a great deal of work remains to be done.

For example, discrepancies still exist between

the standard of living enjoyed by urban Poles and the conditions faced by those in the more rural areas of the country. One major area being focused on for development is the nation's highway system. An ambitious program, launched in 2000 and slated to be completed by 2005, is aimed at building modern highways to connect rural areas to Poland's major transportation and distribution centers. Not only will this increase the quality of life in rural areas by expanding access to goods and services, but a solid system of roadways will enable land transport of goods for manufacture to be achieved more quickly and inexpensively.

Communications are another area where changes are being made. The fixed line telephone system is relatively sophisticated, and service is available nationwide. Current plans are in motion to expand the availability of cellular phone service and to increase competition within that industry. Also the postal system is undergoing a major overhaul, and private postal companies are now in competition with the government-run service. The number of personal computers, while lower than the European average, is on the rise. Internet use is widespread. Poland is seeking to implement plans whereby citizens will be able to access the Internet via the power system, making it the third country in Europe (behind Germany and Switzerland) to do so. The government is also making government services accessible via the Internet, eliminating the need for a costly paper-based bureaucracy.

As a member of the EU, Poland will be able to access millions of dollars in additional funding provided to develop an infrastructure in Poland that is comparable to the rest of Europe. The funds are allocated to help address the economic and social inequalities between the richest and poorest EU nations. This money will be used to support agriculture, build new roads and bridges, improve health-care and social welfare programs, and improve environmental conditions. All these improvements are designed to promote continued foreign investment.

The Poles can also apply to the EU for millions in research dollars. The EU is a source of funding for all types of scientific investigation. Large sums of money are available to promote the development of sustainable agriculture, alternative energy sources, and medicine. Funds will also be available for environmental cleanup and preservation. Although Poland has set aside large areas of its land to be used as sanctuaries and nature preserves, greater funding is needed to ensure enforcement of new laws and to guarantee corporate compliance with new pollution regulations.

Looking Forward

While a few concerns over their sovereignty and national interests remain, there is little doubt that EU membership will greatly improve the standard of living, economic security, and influence of Poland on world affairs. The availability of EU funds for building a more stable infrastructure and a favorable climate for foreign investment are helping to drive a steady recovery from the poverty that marked Poland's years as a communist state. The few drawbacks to Polish membership in the EU are far outweighed by the potential benefits.

Teatr Wieki in Warsaw

A Calendar of Polish Festivals

Poland celebrates many religious, historical, and nonreligious holidays. Food, fun, music, and dancing are integral parts of most Polish festivals. Most public holidays are based on historical events or Roman Catholic holidays.

January: January 1 is a public holiday. The **Nowy Rok**, or New Year's festivities, traditionally include champagne and fireworks. As a public holiday, Poles enjoy this day as a time free from work to enjoy the company of family and friends.

March/April: Easter Week may fall in March or April, and the festival is celebrated throughout the country. **Easter Sunday** is the religious holiday, with a focus on worship and family. It is often celebrated with a large meal. **Easter Monday** is a public holiday, and many festivals occur on this day. Traditional courtship rituals, thought to go back to pagan times, are also observed on this day. Some of these include boys sneaking into a girl's bedroom and dousing her with a bucket of cold water, or girls being slapped on the legs with specially made switches. These switches, usually hand woven of willow and decorated with ribbon, are made by the boy for his intended. Both customs are thought to have originated as ways to promote fertility.

May: May Day is celebrated on May 1, and is intentionally not known as Labor Day, as it was during the communist era. May 3, **Constitution Day**, commemorates the first Polish constitution, drafted May 3, 1791. Both days are public holidays, with most Poles off of work. Because the two holidays are close together, many employers also give their employees May 2 off as well. This means that when the weekend falls favorably, Poles can enjoy five days free from work. This is commonly known as "the Picnic." The seventh Sunday after Easter, known as **Pentecost Sunday**, also commonly falls in May and is considered a public holiday. May 26 is **Mother's Day**.

June: Catholics in Poland celebrate **Corpus Christi**. Celebrated on the ninth Thursday after Easter, this holiday originated as a Roman Catholic holiday and is now recognized as a public holiday where all Poles are off work.

August: The Catholic festival celebrating **Assumption Day** occurs on August 15. This holiday is Roman Catholic in origin but is now an official public holiday for all Poles.

November: All Saints' Day on November 1 is an important religious holiday in certain parts of the country. People remember and honor the dead on this day, often gathering with family and friends for a meal before traveling to decorate the graves of loved ones. **Independence Day** is an important Polish holiday, celebrated by concerts, festivals, and fireworks. Having won their freedom so recently, the Polish people are very patriotic and eager to celebrate this special day.

December: Christmas in Poland is a two-day celebration. While various holiday festivities occur throughout the month of December, December 25 and December 26 are the official public holidays. Families gather together to worship, celebrate, share a meal, and exchange gifts.

Klopsiki w smietanie (Polish meatballs)

This traditional Polish dish features meatballs in a creamy sauce.

Makes 6 servings

Ingredients
1 kaiser roll
1/2 cup milk
1 pound ground beef
1/4 pound ground pork
1 egg
1 small onion, grated
2–3 tablespoons oil
1/4 cup sour cream
2 tablespoons flour
chives, chopped
salt and pepper to taste

Directions
Let kaiser roll sit overnight, until it is hard. Soak roll in 1/2 cup milk until mixture is soggy. Mash with a fork. Combine ground meat, raw egg, and onion with bread mixture. Mix all ingredients well, and add salt and pepper to taste. Roll into golf-ball-sized meatballs. In a frying pan coated with oil, brown meatballs on all sides. Transfer browned meatballs to a baking pan, add 2 tablespoons water, and bake at 325° for 30 minutes. Remove pan from oven and drain drippings. Mix pan drippings with flour and sour cream. Pour mixture back over meatballs and bake for five more minutes. Garnish with freshly chopped chives. For a traditional Polish dinner, serve with mashed potatoes and beets.

Mizeria (Cucumber Salad)

A traditional Polish side dish for summer.

Serves 6–8

Ingredients
3 large cucumbers, chilled
salt and pepper to taste
1 teaspoon sugar
1 teaspoon lemon juice
3/4 cup sour cream
chopped dill for garnish

Directions
Peel and thinly slice cucumbers. Sprinkle with salt, pepper, sugar, and chopped dill. Toss lightly with lemon juice until cucumbers are evenly coated. Add sour cream and mix. Serve immediately.

Jajka w pomidorkach (Eggs Inside Tomatoes)

Another simple Polish side dish.

Serves 8

Ingredients
4 small, firm tomatoes (must be slightly larger than an egg)
4 hard-boiled eggs, peeled
1 package sliced deli ham
3/4 cup mayonnaise
2 teaspoons brown mustard
1/4 teaspoon each of salt and pepper
1 teaspoon lemon juice

Directions
Cut tomatoes in half. Cut each egg in half lengthwise. Scoop out the center of each tomato so that one egg half will fit snugly inside, yolk facing up. Cut 8 slices of ham into narrow shreds, and heap these on top of the stuffed tomatoes. Combine the remaining ingredients to make a sauce, and pour on top of the stuffed tomatoes.

PROJECT AND REPORT IDEAS

Maps

- Make a map of the eurozone, and create a legend to indicate key manufacturing industries throughout the EU.
- Create an export map of Poland using a legend to represent all the major products exported by Poland. The map should clearly indicate all of Poland's major industries.

Reports

- Write a brief report on Poland's automobile industry.
- Write a report on Poland's role within the EU.
- Write a brief report on any of the following historical events: World War I, World War II, the fall of communism.

Biographies

Write a one-page biography on one of the following:

- Lech Walesa
- Frédéric Chopin
- Marie Sklodowska Curie
- Pope John Paul II

Journal

- Imagine you are an exchange student studying in Poland. Write a journal describing your experiences, the types of food you might eat, the places you would visit, and the types of things you would do for entertainment.
- Read more about composer Frédéric Chopin. Imagine you are Frédéric Chopin, and like many Poles your age, you are unhappy about the foreign rule of your land. Write a journal about your life and how your love for your country inspires your music.

Projects

- Learn the Polish expressions for simple words such as hello, good day, please, thank you. Try them on your friends.
- Make a calendar of your country's festivals and list the ones that are common or similar in Poland. Are they celebrated differently in Poland? If so, how?
- Go online or to the library and find images of Gothic churches. Create a model of one.
- Make a poster promoting Polish tourism.
- Make a list of all the rivers, lakes, seas, and cities that you have read about in this book and indicate them on a map of Poland.
- Find a Polish recipe other than the ones given in this book, and ask an adult to help you make it. Share it with members of your class.

Group Activities

- Debate: One side should take the role of Poland and the other France. France's position is that EU should adopt a supranational approach, while Poland will speak in favor of the intergovernmental mode.
- Role play: Reenact a nonviolent demonstration organized by Solidarity.

CHRONOLOGY

966	Mieszko I receives the title of duke and is the first to institute central rule in Poland. Poland begins to convert to Roman Catholicism.
1025	The Kingdom of Poland is established.
1385	The Kingdom of Poland-Lithuania is created.
1569	The Sejm is created.
1795	Poland is divided by three different states in the last of three partitions.
1914	World War I begins.
1918	Poland is reestablished as an independent nation.
1939	Germany invades Poland, and World War II begins.
1945	Allies defeat Germany in World War II.
1945	Soviets institute a communist government in Poland.
1980	Solidarity is formed.
1988	The Communist Party begins formal negotiations with Solidarity.
1990	The communist secretary general resigns, and Lech Walesa is elected president.
1999	Poland joins NATO.
2004	Poland joins the EU.

FURTHER READING/INTERNET RESOURCES

Corona, Laurel. *Poland*. Farmington Hills, Mich.: Thomson Gale, 2000.

Hasday, Judy L. *Marie Curie: Pioneer on the Frontier of Radioactivity*. Berkeley Heights, N.J.: Enslow Publishers, 2004.

Knab, Sophie Hodorowicz. *Polish Customs, Traditions, and Folklore*. New York: Hippocrene Books, 1996.

Pogonowski, Iwo Cyprian. *Poland: An Illustrated History*. New York: Hippocrene Books, 2000.

Zar, Rose, and Eric A. Kimmel. *In the Mouth of the Wolf*. Philadelphia, Pa.: Jewish Publication Society, 1997.

Travel Information
www.lonelyplanet.com/destinations/europe/poland/
www.polandtravel.com

History and Geography
www.infoplease.com
www.wikipedia.org

Culture and Festivals
www.cp.settlement.org/english/poland
www.poland.gov.pl

Economic and Political Information
www.cia.gov/cia/publications/factbook/index.html www.poland-info.org
www.polandembassy.org

EU Information
europa.eu.int/

Publisher's note:
The Web sites listed on this page were active at the time of publication. The publisher is not responsible for Web sites that have changed their addresses or discontinued operation since the date of publication. The publisher will review and update the Web-site list upon each reprint.

FOR MORE INFORMATION

Polish Embassy
2640 16th St. NW
Washington, DC, 20009
Tel.: 202-234-3800

Polish National Tourist Office
5 Marine View Plaza
Hoboken, NJ 07030
Tel.: 201-420-9910
Fax: 201-584-9153

Embassy of the United States in Warsaw
Aleje Ujazdowskie 29/31
00-540 Warsaw Poland
Tel.: +48-22/504-2000

European Union
Delegation of the European Commission to the United States
2300 M Street, NW
Washington, DC 20037
Tel.: 202-862-9500
Fax: 202-429-1766

GLOSSARY

appeasement: The political strategy of pacifying a potentially hostile country by granting them some things that they want in the hope of avoiding war.

autonomous: Able to act independently.

autonomy: Political independence and self-government.

blocs: Unified groups of countries.

capital: Wealth in the form of property or money.

civil liberty: A basic right guaranteed to a citizen by law.

coalition: A temporary union between two or more groups.

compulsory: Required.

concessions: Privileges, rights, or kindnesses that are given to an individual or group in view of special circumstances.

conservation: The preservation, management, and care of natural and cultural resources.

conservative: favoring traditional rules and values; typically opposing change.

continental: Typical of the interiors of the large continents of the Northern Hemisphere.

Crusades: Military expeditions made by European Christians between the eleventh and twelfth centuries to recapture areas taken by Muslim forces.

deported: Forced someone from his or her country.

dissidents: People who publicly disagree with an established political or religious system or organization.

émigré: Someone who leaves his or her native country to live in another country.

excise: A type of tax on domestic goods.

exile: Unwilling absence from one's own country.

feudal system: The legal and social system that existed in medieval Europe, in which vassals held land from lords in exchange for military service.

geothermal: Produced by the heat in the interior of the Earth.

gross domestic product (GDP): The total of all goods and services produced in a country minus the net income from investments in other countries.

homogeneous: Having a uniform composition or structure.

hunter-gatherers: Members of a society in which people live by hunting and gathering only, with no crops or livestock raised for food.

infrastructure: Large-scale public systems and services such as roads and utilities that are necessary for economic activity.

intellectuals: Those with a highly developed ability to reason and understand, especially if well educated and interested in activities involving serious mental effort.

intermittent: From time to time.

liberalizing: Freeing.

market economy: An economy where prices and wages are determined primarily by the market and the law of supply and demand rather than by government regulation.

medieval: Pertaining to the Middle Ages in Europe.

Middle Ages: The period in European history between antiquity and the Italian Renaissance.

nationalism: A feeling of extreme devotion to one nation and its interests about all others.

Neanderthals: Extinct subspecies of humans who lived in Europe, northern Africa, and western Asia in the early Stone Age.

neutral: Not belonging to or favoring any side in a dispute.

nobles: Those belonging to an aristocratic social or political class.

nonaggression treaties: Official agreements between countries promising not to attack one another.

parliament: A house of government.

peasantry: peasants as a class in society.

popularly: By the general public, not a select few.

privatization: The act of transferring to private ownership an economic enterprise or public utility that has been under state ownership.

Protestant Reformation: The sixteenth-century movement to reform the Catholic Church in Western Europe.

ratified: Officially approved.

recession: A period of decline in economic activity, but not lasting as long as a depression.

referendum: A vote by the whole of an electorate on a specific question or questions put to it by a government or similar body.

Renaissance: The period of European history from the fourteenth through the sixteenth centuries marking the end of the Middle Ages and characterized by major cultural and artistic changes.

reneged: Went back on a promise or commitment.

romanticism: Having romantic inclinations.

satellite state: A country completely under the control of another.

scorched-earth: A policy of destroying crops or buildings, especially by burning, that might be useful to an advancing army.

solidarity: Harmony of interests and responsibilities among members of a group.

sovereignty: Supreme authority.

stagnancy: A state of inactivity.

subsidized: Gave money to someone or something in the form of a government grant to help it continue to function.

sustainable: Using natural resources without destroying the ecological balance of a particular area.

tariff: A tax levied by the government on goods, usually imports.

underground: Done in secret.

vernacular: The everyday language of a country's people.

Western: Typical of countries of Europe and North and South America whose culture and society are influenced by Greek and Roman traditions and Christianity.

INDEX

PICTURE CREDITS

Corel: pp. 16–17, 19, 20, 27, 29, 30, 32–33, 49, 50

Used with permission of the European Communities: pp. 52–53, 55, 58, 61, 62

Photos.com: pp. 10–11, 13, 14, 23, 24, 35, 36, 38–39, 40, 41, 44, 46–47, 56, 64, 66–67, 69, 70, 72

BIOGRAPHIES

AUTHOR

Heather Docalavich first developed an interest in the history and cultures of Eastern Europe through her work as a genealogy researcher. She currently resides in Hilton Head, South Carolina, with her four children.

SERIES CONSULTANTS

Ambassador John Bruton served as Irish Prime Minister from 1994 until 1997. As prime minister, he helped turn Ireland's economy into one of the fastest-growing in the world. He was also involved in the Northern Ireland Peace Process, which led to the 1998 Good Friday Agreement. During his tenure as Ireland's prime minister, he also presided over the European Union presidency in 1996 and helped finalize the Stability and Growth Pact, which governs management of the euro. Before being named the European Commission Head of Delegation in the United States, he was a member of the convention that drafted the European Constitution, signed October 29, 2004.

The European Commission Delegation to the United States represents the interests of the European Union as a whole, much as ambassadors represent their countries' interests to the U.S. government. Matters coming under European Commission authority are negotiated between the commission and the U.S. administration.